VOLCANO
TO THE RESCUE!

Adapted by Michael Teitelbaum

Scrat, the sabre-toothed squirrel, zoomed through space on a spaceship. His ship was out of control. It smashed into an asteroid, sending the asteroid hurtling right toward Earth!

Down on Earth, Manny, Ellie, and the rest of their herd learned about the approaching asteroid. If it hit the planet, their Ice Age home would be destroyed.

Luckily, Buck found a stone tablet that he thought could hold the answer to saving their home.

"Every hunded million years or so, the world gets a cosmic cleansing," Buck told them. "The last two asteroids that hit the earth landed in the same spot. I believe that the crash site is where we need to be to stop the new asteroid from colliding with Earth. The site holds the key to finding something from Earth that can knock the asteroid off course."

Despite being scared, the others agreed that Buck's plan was worth a shot. And so, the herd started their march to find the site.

After a long trek, the herd broke through thick, hanging vines. They arrived at the crash site and were amazed by what they saw.

Huge walls of shining, shimmering crystals rose all around them.

"Where *are* we?" asked Manny as he looked around.

"You're in Geotopia!" said Brooke, a sloth with long blond hair.

As the herd looked around, all kinds of amazing-looking animals flew past. Others swung from the vines above.

These were the residents of Geotopia.

"This place is magical," said Shira.

Everyone stepped onto an ice elevator. Up they rose through the gleaming crystal levels of Geotopia. When the elevator stopped, they met the leader of Geotopia, the Shangri-Llama. He was twisting himself into all kinds of yoga positions.

"Shangri-Llama, these visitors have a tablet that says that a light in the sky will destroy the earth and blow us up," said Brooke.

"The light in the sky means us no harm," said the Shangri-Llama. He began twisting himself into some yoga positions. "We are safe here," he added.

"Shangri-Llama, you have to listen to us!" shouted Manny.

"The Llama has spoken," said the Shangri-Llama. It was clear that he was not going to help the herd save the earth.

Buck looked around and picked up a meteor fragment he found on the ground.

Then Crash picked one up. "Hey, look!" he said. "I found one too."

"And so did I!" Eddie said, holding his up.

Suddenly, Crash and Eddie flew through the air, heading right at each other!

KA-RASH!!

The two possums smashed into each other.

"Hey, your meteor is attracted to me!" said Crash.

"No, yours is attracted to *me*!" said Eddie.

Suddenly, it all made sense to Buck. He had made an amazing discovery.

"This whole place is made of magnetic crystals," he said. "That must be why the asteroids always land here! They are literally drawn to this place because of the magnets! I think the answer to saving the world is right under our noses!"

If they could launch magnetic crystals into space, they could pull the asteroid off course!

Sid spotted a beautiful crystal in one of Geotopia's shiny walls. He could not resist it. He reached for it.

"No, Sid, don't do that!" Brooke cried out.

But Sid couldn't help himself. He pulled the crystal from the shiny wall.

KA-RACK! BOOM!

The wall began to crack, then it shattered into a million pieces.

Everyone stared at the huge hole in the wall. In the distance, they saw a tall volcano rising to the sky. Steam and smoke drifted out of the top of the volcano.

"That's it!" Buck cried. "That's the answer we've been looking for. Pent-up energy. The earth's most powerful propulsion device is right in front of us! The volcano. That's our magnet launcher!"

"That's never gonna work," said Diego.

"It will if we seal all the vents around the volcano!" said Buck.

"We need all the crystals here in Geotopia loaded into the volcano," Buck explained. "Then, when the volcano erupts, the crystals will shoot into space. If we're lucky, their magnetic fields will pull the asteroid away from Earth."

"I'm not giving you my crystals!" the Shangri-Llama said. "I need them to rebuild this place."

"These crystals are not yours to keep," said Brooke. "They came from the sky and now it's time to give them back!"

Then Brooke turned to all the members of the herd and the creatures of Geotopia.

"Come on, everybody!" she shouted. "Grab every crystal you can find!"

The herd and the Geotopians gathered up all the crystals they could carry. They marched in a long line to the volcano.

Everyone threw what crystals they had into the volcano and its vents. Wherever steam came out, they pushed in a crystal to keep the steam trapped and build up pressure.

Manny took a large net made out of vines and filled it with crystals. Then he and Julian started dragging the net up the side of the volcano.

One by one, a long line of Geotopia creatures rolled heavy crystals up the volcano. When each one reached the top, they pushed the crystals over the edge, into the opening.

"That's it, my friends, down the hatch!" said Brooke. "Every crystal counts!"

Meanwhile, Buck figured out just how close to the earth the asteroid was at that moment.

"Good news, everyone!" Buck announced. "We're six minutes ahead of its scheduled arrival!"

The whole crowd cheered.

Buck rechecked his calculations.

"Uh, bad news everyone," he said. "We're actually six minutes *behind* schedule."

Manny pointed to a huge crystal near the base of the mountain.

"Double time, everyone," he said. "We need to get that big crystal up into the volcano!"

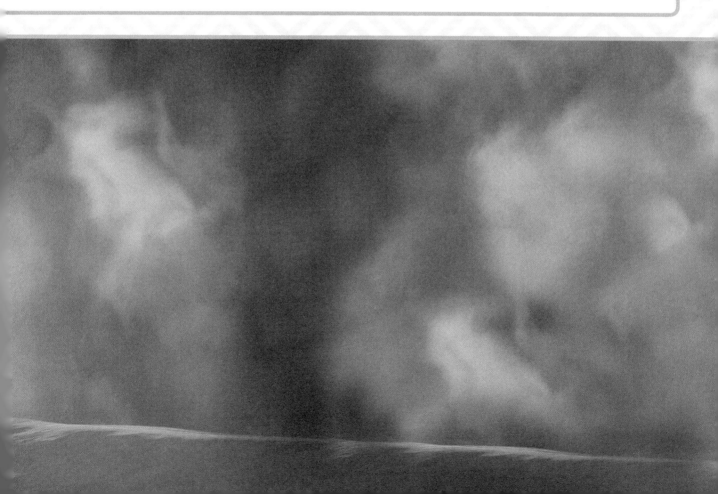

Buck got a family of dino-birds to help.

"Reinforcements have arrived!" shouted Buck.

The dino-birds grabbed the vine net. They flew up, lifting the heavy crystal toward the top of the volcano.

Manny and Julian waited at the top. They watched as Buck guided the dino-birds. In the opening, steaming lava bubbled up. "Okay, let 'er rip!" shouted Buck.

The dino-birds released the net. The giant crystal plunged toward the opening at the top of the volcano.

But it fell short! The crystal began rolling down the side of the volcano.

Manny and Julian ran and caught the rolling crystal. They began pushing it back up the volcano.

"This isn't working," said Manny. "We'll never get the crystal up in time."

"Wait, Manny, I have a plan," said Julian. "We have to let the crystal go."

Manny looked at Julian as if he were crazy.

"You know we're trying to get it *into* the volcano, right?" asked Manny.

"I know it sounds crazy, but just trust me," said Julian.

"Okay, let's do it!" said Manny.

"On my count," said Julian. "One . . . two . . . three!"

They let go of the crystal. It rolled down the side of the volcano, moving faster and faster.

"What are they doing?" cried Shira, as she and the others looked on in disbelief.

When the speeding crystal reached the bottom, it rolled onto a curved section of the volcano. The speed of the rolling boulder and the curve of the volcano sent the crystal flying back up into the air. The crystal flew right to the top, then fell into the volcano.

"It worked!" cried Manny. "Now we just have to wait for the volcano to build up enough pressure to blow."

The volcano continued to rumble and steam, but it didn't erupt.

Manny, Julian, and the others waited.

Just then—*BOOM!* The volcano erupted, sending all the magnetic crystals into space.

Up in space, the cluster of magnetic crystals pulled the asteroid off its course. It sped past Earth, zooming harmlessly off into space.

From inside his spaceship, Scrat watched his planet get saved.

Back at the volcano, everyone was shocked. They couldn't believe their eyes.

"We did it!" cried Manny.

They had saved their home!